FINAL EXIT FOR LAWYERS

MICHAEL VINER

SUSIE DOTAN AND TIM FOLEY CO-CONSPIRATORS

DOVE
BOOKS

FIRST EDITION

Illustrations by: Tim Foley
ISBN 0-7871-0241-5

94 95 96 97   10 9 8 7 6 5 4 3 2 1

Other Books by the author:

Final Exit for Cats
Final Exit for Barney
Final Exit for O.J.
Final Exit for Marlon Brando (autobiography)
Final Exit for Anna Nicole Smith (the man I used to be)
Final Exit for Romeo, Juliet and Madonna (a pictorial)
Bridges of Madison County -Memoirs of a dentist
Schindler's Duck - Famous WW2 recipes
Lincoln at Gettysburg - Henry Ford remembers

Rumor has it that they breed under rocks in the hot deserts of California, Nevada and Utah. From there they leave their nests and crawl their way through the underbrush to the rest of the world. Once arriving at their final destinations, they shed their skins, don suits and hang out shingles. They call themselves attorneys, lawyers, or advocates, but they really cannot leave their ancestry too far behind, because when you least expect, they bare their poisonous fangs, and bite down hard.

Their ability to procreate is phenomenal. The world is crawling with an excess of these dangerous creatures, and every year their population multiplies at a horrific rate. So, we decided to stop the propagation of this species. In the following pages, we have demonstrated our solutions to this overwhelming blight. Their final exit.

Tell the ambulance driver to slam on the brakes.

Design a computer program that eliminates the need for all lawyers.

Tell them they absolutely cannot make stupid TV commercials that star themselves.

Revoke their Country Club memberships.

Force them to shop at Target.

Make them tell the absolute truth for an entire month.

Make them all re-take the bar exam on their ten and twenty-year legal anniversaries, and congratulate the one that passes.

Send them helicopter skiing with Christie Brinkley.

Take away their Rolex watches.

Take away their cellular phones.

Make them watch every Perry Mason episode ever made, including the made-for-TV movies.

Make them wear suits made out of 100% polyester.

Inform them the public has more respect and trust in a used car salesman than they do in lawyers.

Relocate their offices to Death Valley.

Force them to live on $100,000 a year.

Tell both sides they can't try their cases in the media.

Take away their golf carts and make them walk the entire 18-hole golf course.

Make them actually read the depositions their clients have given.

Take away their legal pads, and give them paper without lines instead.

Make John Grisham partner.

Tell them they can't use earth-tones and wood to decorate their offices.

Force two lawyers to marry each other, each with a prenuptial agreement in hand.

Force them to be honest in their billable hours.

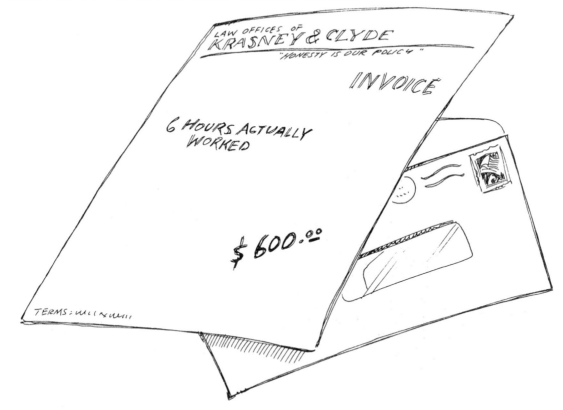

Force them to learn how to use their own computers.

Force them to drive American made cars.

Take away their credit cards and force them to pay with cash.

Make it mandatory that they display their college grades and not just their diplomas.

Force them to recommend this book to all their friends.

The Male of the Species

His most definitive markings are blue or grey pinstripes up and down his body. His neck usually has a tie. He is mostly found anywhere money is present. His behavior varies and cannot be depended on for any kind of consistency. His speech patterns are constructed in such a manner that he is hard to understand in any kind of situation, but is sure to bill you for any conversation you may have had with him, whether or not you understood that you actually had one. The most important things to him, besides winning, are status symbols, which he collects with lust and fervor. He is easy to spot, because he is the one with the flashy car, the flashy girl, and will probably be wearing a Rolex.

Put him in charge of protecting Elvis Presley's musical copyrights.

Cast him in an Oliver Stone movie.

Make him the defense attorney when Marcia Clark is the prosecutor.

Have him join the O.J. Simpson defense team.

Have him represent O.J. Simpson on contingency.

Convince him that handing the keys of his Porsche to the valet parking attendant is perfectly fine.

Make him read the letter he sent to you and then translate it into English.

Send him bungee jumping with a frayed cord.

Send him in to defend Mike Tyson on his appeal — and then lose!

Tell him he has to work 50 weeks a year.

Send him downtown in his Mercedes, wearing his Armani suit with a pocket full of cash, after 10:00 p.m.

Send him white water river rafting in heavy rapids with Meryl Streep.

Send him in to mediate the former Yugoslavia peace talks.

Send him up before a judge who hasn't eaten all day and has low blood sugar.

Take him to visit the shark tank at Sea World.

Have Janet Reno appoint him as special prosecutor in a high profile case.

Send him into court wearing an old Laugh-In tee shirt that says "Here Come Da Judge."

Send him to Singapore to protest the caning of an American citizen with a can of spray paint in his brief case.

Give him a Bullwinkle hat and take him hunting on the opening day of deer season.

Hang him by his suspenders.

Send the thug he got off on a technicality over to his house to commit the same crime.

Take away his unlisted phone number.

Use his inflated ego as a flotation device in a swimming pool.

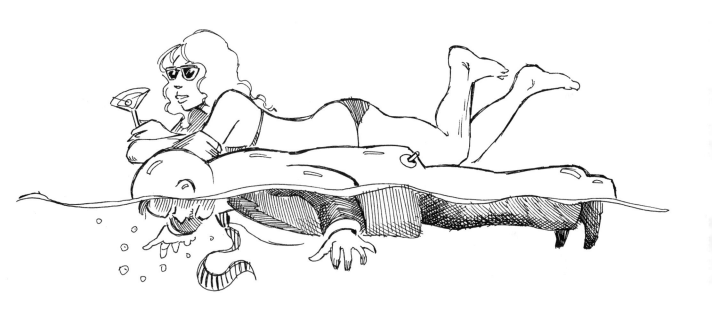

Convince him to aspire to hold a high political office.

Make him run for political office without waging a slander campaign.

Make him change his own flat tire for the very first time without the assistance of the auto club.

Convince him to fly on Aeroflot Airlines the day the pilot is giving his kids flying lessons.

Make him the attorney for Roseanne Barr and Tom Arnold.

Make him choose which one he'll represent for the divorce.

Give him an annual membership to a local gym, and then make sure he uses it

Send him a client who can out-talk him.

Put an "I ♥ lawyers" bumper sticker on his car.

Choke him on his legalese.

Put a Milk-Bone in his hand and tell him to whistle.

Make him Heidi Fleiss' tax attorney.

Give him teenagers who want to join a punk rock and roll band.

Give him a teenage daughter who doesn't know the meaning of the word "NO!"

Have Congressman Dan Rostenkowski make his travel plans and do his mailings.

When he's out of town on a business trip, have him cheat on his wife without any kind of protection.

The Female of the Species

She is a little harder to pick out in a crowd, because it is often hard to tell whether or not she really is a female. With patience, however, you can hear her very discernible cry ("Oh shit I broke a nail!") which will help you in establishing her gender. Once having established that she is indeed a she, it is highly advisable that one take the same precautionary measures when approaching her, as you would the male of the species. The female of the species, while quite new on the law scene, has been making strident advances in the short time she has evolved, and is quickly catching up to the same predatory levels as her male counterparts. In some cases, she can even be more vicious, because her lust for flashy men is nonexistent and she therefore has less distractions from her set goal, which is to put you in the poorhouse.

Force her to look
like a woman.

Force her to buy her clothes "off the rack."

Hire her into a firm where all the partners are men.

Make her the attorney for Bill Clinton's defense against Paula Jones, and then send her to interview him in the Lincoln room of the White House.

Tell her what salary her male counterparts are actually making in comparison to hers.

Send her up before a female judge on a day when they're both suffering from PMS.

Have her teach a civil procedures class at any law school.

Make her fly coach.

Submit her name and phone number to every telemarketing company out there and instruct them to phone after 9:00 p.m.

Then sell her name and address to every junk mail house in the country.

Have her step into an elevator alone after 7:00 p.m. filled with "potential clients."

Send her to a party where all the guests want free legal advice.

Tell her she looks much better with a tan and hand her a years membership to the George Hamilton Tanning Salon.

Tell her it's easy to find a job straight out of law school.

Cancel her manicure appointment.

Hide her blow dryer.

Make her wear her hair like Leslie Abramson.

Make her jog every morning to stay fit.

Make her the lawyer for Dove.

ABOUT THE AUTHOR:

Michael Viner was first discovered in Yellowstone National Park where he had evidently been left behind. He was raised by wolves, but quickly adapted to civilization and in fact attended Harvard University where he achieved a straight "A" average until tragedy struck. On his way to his graduation ceremony, he was run over while chasing a car . . . but he's doing better now. . . thank you.

ABOUT THE CO-AUTHORS:

Susie Dotan is best known by those who cruise the Sunset Strip, for her tight cycling outfit and her ability to make friends quickly.

Tim Foley is the talented cartoonist and portrait artist whose work is often featured on America's Most Wanted, though not in connection with his drawings.